Taming Molly

Sign up at www.LizKellyBooks.com
to be alerted when new books are released.

TAMING **MOLLY**

HEROES OF HENDERSON: BOOK 2.5

A DuVal Cousins Quickie

Published by Kelly Girl Productions
©Copyright 2014 Liz Kelly
Cover design by Tammy Kearly

ISBN: 978-0-9889838-9-2

This book is a work of fiction. The characters, events and places portrayed
in this book are products of the author's imagination and are either
fictitious or are used fictitiously. Any similarity to real persons, living or
dead, is purely coincidental and not intended by the author.

For more information on the author and her works, please see www.
LizKellyBooks.com.

For all my girl cousins.
Especially the wild ones.
You know who you are.

CHAPTER ONE

Big Jim DuVal loved his firstborn daughter. Hell, he loved all his daughters. Equally. But the moment that first one, his Molly, was born, she captured his heart with a fierceness he didn't know existed. With that thick patch of rosy hair and those blue-green eyes, she looked just like her momma, and he figured he must be the luckiest man alive to have two beautiful females carrying his name.

So he doted on them both, chuckling at his wife's frustration when their baby daughter crawled away during her diaperings to hide her naked tushy behind his legs. And then later, when as a toddler Molly'd scramble into his lap laughing so cute he'd just have to join in as she'd tear off her clothes tossing everything pink and ruffly to the floor. She'd even kick off her shoes and socks, preferring to be unhampered by any clothing as she scampered around the house naked and giggling.

By the time Molly was four, she was prone to pulling her shirt up over her head in public, exposing her chest and her little round belly. But Big Jim just laughed and took those opportunities to nuzzle up to his exasperated wife's ear and whisper that Molly reminded him a lot of her.

His little darling grew up sweet and kind. All of Molly's teachers claimed she was the one who would befriend the new kid in the class and pick the less fortunate athletes for her kickball team. She insisted on inviting all the girls to her birthday so no one's feelings got hurt. She was as beautiful on the inside as she was becoming on the outside, and he was so proud of all of it that he paid zero attention to his wife's concerns. All of his wife's carryings-on about Molly's predilection to short shorts and cropped tops didn't faze him. In his opinion, she looked adorable in whatever she wore.

But Big Jim remembered well one hot summer day right before Molly entered eighth grade. The day when he got an inkling of what his wife had been frettin' about all those years. That day spent around Henderson Country Club's pool with his beautiful family opened his eyes…but good. Because when he tracked the appreciative stares from a bunch of young yahoos to a gaggle of pretty girls chatting around the snack bar, he saw it.

His sweet little Molly stood half a head taller than the rest of those young ladies, and her baby-girl belly had somehow turned into a tiny tucked-in waist. From her lean, shapely legs to her strawberry-blond curls, his darlin' Molly had suddenly blossomed into a voluptuous young woman.

Just like her mother.

Wearing the skimpiest bikini ever known to man.

He turned to his darling wife who was stretched out on the lounge chair beside him, planning to complain for the first time ever about what their Molly was wearing. But he quickly bit his tongue because there was nothing Molly was showing off that his beautiful bride wasn't. And that's when it hit him. Molly was indeed just like her mother.

Lord Jesus.

That's when his own teenage years began flashing before his eyes, and Big Jim started backpedaling. Fast.

That evening, once the girls were in bed, he opened a nice bottle of wine and set out to have a heart-to-heart chat with his wife. He suggested that the time had come for her to have a conversation with Molly about dressing appropriately, about propriety, and about the importance of maintaining a good reputation, especially in a small, gossipy town like Henderson. He rambled on, stating his case and his concerns for their eldest daughter and her lovely figure, until he noticed the stony silence and stiff posture emanating from the woman sitting next to him on the back porch.

Lori Bamberger DuVal, his bride of fifteen years at the time, didn't mince words. No, she reminded him that her skimpily clad figure and questionable reputation were exactly what had attracted Big Jim to her in the first place. Then she reminded him that he was no damn saint himself. And if he thought she would ever play the hypocrite by openly lying to their daughters about her own behavior in high school—when in this small town they would likely find out anyway—then he had another thing comin'.

She'd tried to warn him, she said. All these years he'd been laughing at Molly's nudie-patootie antics, saying she was just like her mother. Well, the chickens had finally come home to roost. And as she stomped by Big Jim on the way to locking him out of their bedroom, she suggested he might want to call his father-in-law and apologize, now that the shoe was on the other foot.

Like hell.

Big Jim didn't call his father-in-law. He called the best darn pool contractor he could afford and had a luxurious inground pool installed. If his wife and daughters wanted to wear skimpy bikinis, fine. They could damn well do it in their own backyard.

He acknowledged that it sort of backfired on him when they all started sunbathing topless.

Whatever. He just built a taller fence.

Two years later, he actually did call his poor father-in-law and apologize for his own earlier behavior. This came after spending half the night tracking down Molly and dragging her shirtless body out of the back seat of some handsy football player's truck. Big Jim's apology only served to fuel the fire by making Molly her grandfather's favorite—which he proved by giving her a farm-girl Ford on her sixteenth birthday.

Damn fool.

After that it seemed Big Jim spent his weekends putting out fires where Molly was concerned. Oh, he still loved her to distraction. Was still as proud as any father could be. She was studious enough for him and particularly brilliant in her artistic pursuits. She was sweet to all her little cousins who idolized her. She had plenty of friends he didn't mind hosting at his home for overnights or treating to dinner at the Club from time to time.

But that's where his hospitality ended. When it came to Molly's dates, Big Jim made it his mission to scare the livin' hell out of them.

Which backfired of course, because then Molly wouldn't let them pick her up at home. She'd trot off and meet them under the cover of darkness, as far as he could tell.

There was one good screaming match between the two of them during her high school years that broke his heart in all kinds of places. The next morning, he decided to throw in the towel. He told her he loved her and always would, no matter what. Then he backed off and spent twice the time on his knees praying that she'd make it through high school and into college before any real shit hit the fan.

It was a challenge when she took off for Mardi Gras after turning eighteen and brought home more beads than any dad need be aware of.

It was tough to shake off the scandal of the Debutante with the Plunging Neckline, when Molly left her age-appropriate escort in the middle of the ball only to be seen the next day getting out of a very distinctive Porsche belonging to an older, notorious Raleigh bachelor.

And then, just before Molly's college graduation from Elon University, the highlight of the annual student art show were the beautiful nudes done in pencil, ink, and oil. One model seemed to be a particular favorite among the art students. Big Jim had to excuse himself from the crowd, pretending he couldn't add one and one.

The truth couldn't be denied. His precious daughter was an exhibitionist and always had been. She was interested in the human body and didn't see a need to cover it up. The fact that she planned her European travels around nude beaches shouldn't have been much of a shock.

Still, there was so much about Molly to love that Big Jim continued to indulge her. Though he had to admit that when she got engaged at the age of twenty-three to a nice kid from an old-school Henderson family, he sighed in big relief.

Until the shit really hit the fan.

CHAPTER TWO

Henderson High School
Two weeks before the Evans-DuVal Wedding

Josh McCourt looked more like a suit-and-tie guy than any sort of assistant athletic coach. His butterscotch hair was businessman short, his shoulders broad but not musclebound. He didn't have the traditional beer belly many coaches carried around, and he liked to keep his phone in a brown leather case attached to his belt. He might not fit into the stereotypical mold of a football coach, especially when he'd never played a day in his life—but right now he was beyond spellbound by the entirety of his first few weeks of football practice.

In all his twenty-eight years, he had never, ever thought about doing something like this. But he had to admit, using his computer skills to come up with a software program for the good of a team gave him new perspective. On everything. Yeah, he was taking to this team thing like a duck takes to water. He with his lone wolf, statistically inclined brain and his makeshift Google glassware. Who would have thought?

After the first two days of practice as assistant to the offensive coordinator, he'd been deemed Coach Razzle by the players.

Coach Razzle! That was cool, right?

The crazy success they were having with his razzle-dazzle pitch-back-and-throw plays, along with his end-around and back-around scramble-'em-all-up plays, was bringing new life to the team.

Of course the defense didn't like him much at the moment because he was making them look like a bunch of clumsy Neanderthals out there. But once the Bulldogs started scoring against other teams, he figured they'd come around okay. At least he hoped that's how it would work out.

Because Henderson's football team hadn't done much lately. The decline came on the heels of the first State Championship win for the Henderson baseball team, causing the town's interest in football to wane and making baseball *the sport* in Henderson. Over the last ten years, the Mighty Bulldogs had consistently lost an average of fifty percent of their football games.

Josh himself had been in high school at the time of the big baseball win. Of course, he hadn't been a student at Henderson then. No, he'd watched it all unfold from Henderson's archrival in the next town over, Oxford. The school that lost to Henderson just before they headed off to the state championship.

Being raised in Oxford wasn't something he shared with his Henderson students. There was no love lost between these two towns when it came to sports and other rivalries. He bet they'd look critically at his strange coaching suggestions and possibly misinterpret his intentions. They might worry that he was over here in Henderson to sabotage the team's efforts, even though he'd been their AP Computer Science teacher going on five years now. He wouldn't be surprised if his loyalties were questioned. It was just that kind of rivalry.

Still, the old Henderson guard had been happy to call on him and his computer skills to do what he could do to get this "Henderson football thing" turned around. That's what Big Jim DuVal, head of the Boosters Club, had said when he'd addressed the entire faculty at the end of last year. "We've got to get our sports teams back on top," he said. "There is no reason we can't have a winning football team and basketball team right along with our illustrious baseball team."

Everyone knew Big Jim had a storied history playing quarterback at Henderson High. Then he went on to have a winning career as a running back at East Carolina. So it was no secret that the overwhelming love for baseball this town had developed had been burning his ass but good. Now Big Jim's own nephew was refusing to play tight end this year, so he could focus solely on his pitching arm as Coach Evans suggested.

Speak of the devil.

Coach Evans came around the corner at a jog and practically banged into Josh as he was opening the training room door.

"Hey, Josh! How's your summer going?" Vance asked, but both men were immediately distracted by the squealing and giggling going on inside the training room. The training room located inside the *boys'* locker room. When they forced the doors open, Josh was secretly glad Vance was there. Because to save his life, Josh would have had no idea how to handle the prevailing situation.

Six boys, all sweaty football players Josh could name, and three pretty young girls dressed in bun-hugging athletic shorts and crop tops—or were they sports bras? Josh never knew the difference—were chasing each other around the weight training equipment slapping hands, pulling ponytails, and generally having a grand ol' time flirting. The fun scrambled to a dead halt when he and Vance stepped through the door, the girls turning bright red and the guys just smirking like they'd been through this before.

"Ladies," Vance said, as he held the door open and let his free arm usher them out of the room. The three of them practically fell over one another, giggling as they pushed through the door.

Once the giggling drifted away, Coach Evans closed the door and turned his attention to the front line of his offense. Man, Josh hoped this wasn't going to end poorly.

"One of those was a DuVal, right?" Vance asked.

Thatcher Douglas nodded his head. "Tinley. The little blonde with the big tits."

Josh heard Vance's heavy sigh. "Okay. That one—with the last name of DuVal—she is now classified as off limits. The other two, whatever. Only not here. Never in here. This is my *office*, for Christ's sake. I don't know why people think it's okay to fool around in my office…." He trailed off, rubbing his chin, looking over at the barely chagrined youths. "What do you think, Josh? A little tough love in the form of circuit training?"

What the F is circuit training?

"Be my guest," Josh said. He allowed his left hand to drift toward the boys hoping Vance would go ahead and…do the honors.

It didn't take long for Vance to demonstrate a six-machine circuit of punishment for Henderson's front line. Once the groans were going full force and the sweat was really flowing, Vance gave Josh a cheeky grin as they stood back overseeing the action. "Should I be feelin' at all bad punishing them for something I would have done back in my day?"

Josh lifted one shoulder in a shrug. "Frankly, I'm feelin' bad that sneakin' a girl into the locker room never occurred to me."

Vance slapped him on the back. "Welcome to the world of sports, where an athlete's one continuous thought is thinkin' about scoring, on and *off* the field."

"I hear ya. One week on the team has certainly opened my eyes."

"How's that?"

Josh shook his head, not really knowing how to put it in words. "It's like I've been livin' my life in self-imposed solitary confinement. Lord, when I was their age, all I did after school was take things apart and then put them back together—computers mostly, but other stuff too—just to figure out how they worked. Then I'd try to make them work faster, or better, with fewer parts. Then I'd see if I could design my own computer to do one thing or another, then…well, you get the picture. Now that I'm working with the football team, I still do the solitary work of designing the program, inputting a specific defensive strategy, layering in whatever stats I have on my offensive players, and then have the computer come up with play options that will run through that particular defense. But when I bring all that to the field, well, I actually don't know what's gonna happen. Because, I have now realized, when you add the human factor into the equation that's when the excitement really begins."

Vance stared at him blankly and then blinked a few times before he said, "You have got to meet Lewis Kampmueller."

"Been working for the man for years. He's a buddy of yours, right?"

"Right."

"Yeah, Lewis wants me to move to New York. Says he'll give me an office at KampApps. But I'm not all that interested in leaving

North Carolina. Besides, I can work in solitary here just as well as there."

Vance chuckled. "Sounds like your days in solitary are numbered."

"I didn't realize how much I'd like the camaraderie. Especially from a group of guys who know next to nothing about physics on paper. But I can tell you this. Their brains and their bodies sure get it out there on the field. Do you know how many mathematical calculations it takes for a quarterback to release a perfect spiral and have it arrive at the exact place and the exact time where a receiver is eventually going to be?"

Vance shook his head. "I honestly have no idea."

"Neither do I," Josh exclaimed. "It's like a miracle. The fact that my plays are working out fifty percent of the time and they've just started learning them?" He shook his head. "I like the human factor. More than I expected."

Just then some pushing, shoving, and cursing broke out among his front line as they shifted from one machine to the next. The physical punishment of a long day out in the summer sun along with the extra burden of circuit training was apparently undoing them.

"How do you like that human factor now?" Vance asked over his shoulder as he headed to break up the brawl. "All right, all right," he shouted, clapping his hands. "That'll do. Hit the showers and then find a whiteboard somewhere and write *I will never bring a girl into Coach Evans' office again*, fifty times. We are done here. Move out."

Josh watched them go. "Are they really gonna do that? Write it out fifty times?"

"Are you fucking nuts? Of course they're not gonna do it. I just wanted to get my point across."

Josh laughed. "Tell me about that DuVal girl. The cute one. Why'd you classify her as off limits?"

Vance shrugged. "I'm friends with Lolly, one of the many, many DuVal cousins running around Henderson. My father is marrying Lolly's mother, Genevra, so I'm feeling a bit protective about all the ladies DuVal right now. And there are a slew of them, I tell you. Lolly worked me up a cheat sheet so I'd be able to figure out who was who at the wedding."

Vance walked over to his desk, grabbed up a sheet of paper, and read. "The DuVal cousins from oldest to youngest. Molly, Lilly, Lucy, Jacey, Lolly, Linley, Vivi, and Tinley. That does not include the one shining DuVal Y chromosome, Henry, who is a starter on my baseball team."

"I hear he's got a good arm and can run fast."

"Yeah, yeah—no. Don't even think about him. You and your crazy computer generated plays are not going to lure my pitcher into a head-bashing, concussion-producing, bone-breaking sport so that he's sittin' on the damn bench come spring."

"Not much of a football fan, are you?" Josh asked.

"Absolutely love it. Just tryin' to protect my championship-winning baseball team."

Josh chuckled. "There's a lot of statistics in baseball. Maybe I can find a way to help out your team this spring."

Vance looked up, pleased. "Maybe you can at that."

"And being as you are close to all those DuVal ladies, maybe you can do something for me."

Vance looked skeptical. "What would that be?"

"I want you to fix me up with the wild one. That first one. The oldest."

"Molly?"

"Yes, Molly. She won't remember, but she was sweet to me back in high school when I came over to compete with Henderson High's *It's Academic* team."

"Molly DuVal was never on any academic team," Vance assured him.

"No. But when I got the directions to the auditorium wrong, she noticed. She introduced herself and showed me the way. Even wished me good luck."

"You remembered her? From that?"

"A pretty girl, payin' attention to me? Of course I remembered her."

"Trust me, even if she still lived in town, Molly DuVal is not your type."

"Perfect. Because I am no longer interested in my type. I've dated a lot of my type. Nice physics majors, brilliant mathematicians, and pretty little bookworms. None of them made me want to take them apart to see how they work, if you get my drift. These last few weeks have woken me up to a piece of myself I didn't realize existed. I like being social. I like being a part of a team, and I like taking charge. I like contributing and getting feedback in the form of a high five. Who knew? Being one of the assistant coaches has made me realize I need to get out more. Because if I can find a reason to enjoy being around a bunch of sweaty, grunting, musclebound jocks, I'm pretty sure there's a lot of other stuff outside my computer lair I'm going to enjoy, too. You're Vance Evans. You know a lot of women. Introduce me to one who is willing to sneak into a locker room and let me chase her around the equipment."

Vance choked out a laugh.

"What?"

"You sure know how to pick 'em."

"What do you mean?"

"I mean, Molly DuVal crawled all over me back before I even knew what a hickey was, much less what to do with all those soft, round, sweet-smelling parts she was pressing up against me. She will be the one taking *you* apart, and there is no guarantee she'll bother putting you back together."

"I'll take my chances," Josh said. He felt the big grin splitting his face at the same time a part of his brain was blinking *tilt*.

Vance scrutinized Josh as he rubbed a hand over his jaw. "The fact is I sort of had a hand in Molly moving out of town a few years back. Lately I've been feeling a little guilty about that, so I'm not willing to do all that much here. However, there is a high statistical probability that she will show up for her aunt's wedding two weeks from Saturday. What I can do is get you on that guest list. I'll point her out during the reception. There will be a band, food, and alcohol, along with a lot of flowers and a very romantic setting. Whatever the hell happens after that is all up to you."

Josh licked his lips. "Done."

CHAPTER THREE

Molly DuVal stood tapping the engraved wedding invitation against her fingertips. She ran a thumb over the lovely loopy handwriting covering the attached sticky note.

Molly, it would mean the world to me if you were able to attend. I've spoken to your father. He is eager for your attendance as well.
Love, Aunt Gen

Whether Aunt Genevra had spoken to her father or not, Molly had no intention of missing her aunt's wedding. She'd been missing out on way too much over the last several years, and right now she was full-out missin' every last one of the crazy DuVal clan—but most especially her cousins.

As much as her father hated her use of the word *banned*, after she'd made the rather spectacular but unfortunate choice of breaking off her engagement to Tyler Jackson by running away for a weekend with Vance Evans, he was the one who had strongly suggested that she move her gossip-feeding shenanigans outside of Henderson.

Far outside of Henderson.

She thought her father was merely being dramatic until the ultimate blow was handed down from Henderson's upper crust. No doubt following the lead of Tyler's grandmother, Evie Jackson, the secret society decided that Molly's beloved cousin, Jacey DuVal, would not be invited to make her debut. Jacey, who was the girliest of all the cousins, was devastated and Jacey's mother, Aunt Charlotte, was beyond consolation.

And it was all Molly's fault.

Tearfully she'd agreed with her father, apologized to Jacey, Aunt Charlotte, and Uncle Jeb, and then snuck out of town.

Molly had been socially banned from Henderson, but not entirely exiled. She'd gone home for Thanksgiving and Christmas, participating in all the DuVal family rituals. Her parents, sisters, and cousins, even Jacey, were always happy to see her. But leaving the house and going out partying with them and her old friends over the holidays? Not a good idea, her dad told her.

And it probably wasn't.

Because Molly knew herself well. Now that she'd been working and living in Raleigh for five years, she'd figured out a few things. Family and friends were just about everything. And most of hers lived and played in Henderson. Or at least, that is where they gathered from time to time.

Sure, she would arrange the *DuVal-Cousins-Take-On-Raleigh Night* each year. Molly, Lilly, Lucy, Jacey, Lolly, Tipi, Vivi, and Tinley would gather in her tiny apartment for drinks and dinner, catching up before heading out on the town. Standing back and watching her younger sisters and cousins take over the dance floor at The Charlie Horse or Solas made her wonder how she was the one with the bad rap. It certainly wasn't like she was dragging a pack of wallflowers around town. Oh, she was happy to see them all having fun. She just wished she were still like them. Fun.

Because something had truly been crushed over the years since she was forced to move out of Henderson.

At first, her friends would come and spend the weekend. They'd go out and really raise hell on Fayetteville Street and Glenwood South. She wondered why she hadn't moved to Raleigh earlier.

But then life started to happen. Everybody took on real-life jobs and the time between visits stretched longer and longer as everyone's responsibilities increased. It wasn't like Molly could reciprocate with the travel and make the drive home to Henderson to play. She had to wait for them to come to her.

Rent came due every month and not just for her apartment, but for the tiny artist's co-op space and equipment she used to indulge in her crafts. Though she eventually made some new and interesting friends through the artistic connections in town, it still felt lonely.

Her hours at the art gallery weren't long, so she began focusing on her ceramics. Never one to do anything casually, she ended up spending a lot of time in quiet solitude, throwing clay. Eventually she started spending her extra cash on art supplies rather than club cover charges and drinks.

Perhaps that was the silver lining in all of this.

Because her pottery was now selling. And selling at outrageous prices from the gallery in which she worked. Which was really just a happy accident—because in a panic, Lana Bristol, the store owner, had strategically placed a few of Molly's brightly colored, hand-painted, and glazed pottery pieces in the empty spaces when store merchandise was low. The crazy prices they'd slapped on her items were simply in keeping with the range the fine art store was known for. So when the first piece was purchased not two days later, Molly and Lana spent the afternoon in total shock, laughing over the sale.

The fact that patrons had the opportunity to meet the artist seemed to be a bonus and a selling point. After they conversed with Molly, they'd want her to sign the bottom of her piece with a Sharpie right next to her signature stamp. If they were purchasing it as a gift, they'd ask her to personalize the plate or vase with her Sharpie. Then they'd special order her pieces in certain colors and sizes, which Molly was only too happy to fulfill at a premium. And just when Molly thought things could not get better, calls began coming in from other art galleries in other cities, asking for information about ordering her pottery.

It was all quite thrilling. And so very, very lonely. Because no one she cared about had any idea this was going on. It just wasn't something she could bring up to her starving artist friends. "Guess what? I made real money this month doing exactly what I love to do."

No.

Nor had she told her long-distance friends and loved ones about her success. That she wanted to share in person.

But she had a plan. A plan to get herself moved back home. And Aunt Genevra's wedding provided the perfect opportunity.

CHAPTER FOUR

Molly was a little flustered that the parking valet was at her door so quickly, opening it up and helping her out of her little truck. She'd anticipated parking in one of the many fields surrounding Hale Evans' mansion. Apparently that wouldn't do for Mr. Evans' guests because everywhere she looked there were smartly dressed young men providing valet parking from the front door of the Evans' estate, or readying golf carts to drive guests to the site of the outdoor wedding.

She asked for a moment, slipping off her worn out flip-flops and donning her emerald green heels. Then she grabbed up the pretty tulle overskirt she hadn't wanted to wrinkle on the long drive from Raleigh. She wrapped it around her waist, fastening the satin emerald bow over her belly button. It was what turned the sexy, little body-hugging green dress into a lovely confection even old Evie Jackson would approve of. Between her poofy tulle skirt, her high heels, and the French twist she'd pulled her blonde hair into, her ladylike appearance could not be faulted.

Just like she'd planned.

The last thing she grabbed, in addition to her matching clutch purse, was the wedding gift she'd made especially for Aunt Genevra and her new husband. It was an original "Molly DuVal Piece," which was starting to mean something in North Carolina, and there was only one like it. She knew her aunt loved to cook, so she hoped what was lying inside the large, beautifully wrapped, pizza box would suit her.

"Need help with that?" her sister Lucy said, snatching the box out of her hands. One look at her youngest sister made Molly want to melt with joy. They hugged around the box as best they could and were soon pounced on by Lilly, their middle sister, and Jacey and Vivi, their cousins.

"We are so happy you came," one of them exclaimed, getting in on the hug. The five of them huddled together, jumping up and down with excitement over the wedding, over Molly being there for it, and over just being back together.

"I'm sure Lolly is with Aunt Gen, but where are Linley and Tinley?"

"Savin' us seats, of course," Lucy said. "Let's squeeze into one of these golf carts and head up." Lucy handed over Molly's gift to one of the staff who stood at the front door for that very purpose, and then all five of them started to crowd onto a golf cart meant for three and a driver.

"Wait," Molly said, balking. "Y'all go ahead. Lucy and I will take the next cart."

"But why?" Lucy complained. "We can all fit. Here, just sit on my lap."

Molly bit her lip, torn. There wasn't anything she'd rather do than climb on board with her sisters and her cousins. But she knew it didn't fit with her plans for the day. She couldn't be seen arriving in a passel of silly girls, laughing too loud and having too much fun before the wedding even commenced. No, she had to look the part of the reformed party girl. Project the image that the eldest DuVal cousin had finally grown up and had her head on straight. There would be no sitting on laps today. Prim and proper were the keywords for this event.

"Y'all go on. We'll be right behind you," Molly said, grabbing up Lucy's hand and dragging her to the next golf cart. She and Lucy arranged themselves in the back, and at Lucy's expectant look, Molly confessed everything.

"I'm lonely, and I want to come home."

"Thank God," Lucy breathed.

"In order to do that, I have to show Daddy I'm over the running-around-with-boys thing. Today I want him and everybody else to see that I have matured and will no longer be fodder for the Henderson gossips."

Lucy looked a little stupefied. "Well, that just sounds boring. I think I speak for the entire family and the rest of your friends too when I say we don't want any dumbed-down version of Molly DuVal back. We want the real thing. Good Lord, this town is dying enough already. Please don't change your spots to try to fit in. Just be yourself and breathe some life back into this place. Besides, Tinley is causing more trouble than you could have ever dreamed up, so…whatever… it's all relative—literally."

The two sisters laughed at that, holding on to the sides of the cart as they were transported up a steep hill to the beautiful football-field-sized tent glistening in the sunlight.

"Wow," Molly said.

"It's air-conditioned," Lucy responded. "I swear Aunt Gen has fallen into a pot of gold with Mr. Evans. He's better looking than Vance and sure knows how to throw a party."

"I haven't seen Vance since he helped me break my engagement."

"Is that how we're remembering it now? Vance helped you break off your engagement? Not that you ran off for one last fling with Mr. Great in the Sack?"

"You say tomato…."

"I'll say anything you want as long as you move back to town and share an apartment with me. I am too old to be living at home."

"Just run interference with Vance, okay? I'm not interested in picking up where we left off."

"Yeah, well as I understand it, he's now Lolly's best friend and there is some chick from out of town he's working hard to impress, so you're safe there."

"Good."

Lucy hopped off the cart as soon as it stopped, but Molly waited for their driver to give her a hand down onto the grass. Luckily, there'd been little rain, so her heels didn't dig into the ground. The two of them met up with their cousins and wandered down the rose-strewn aisle where Tinley and Linley held a whole row of seats for them. Right behind all of their parents.

It was the sort of spectacle Molly had hoped to avoid. Her mom and dad and her aunts and uncles fawned over her return to Henderson—right in the middle of everyone. There wasn't one eye turned in another direction as Molly was embraced, kissed, and welcomed back with literal open arms.

So sue her. It felt good.

CHAPTER FIVE

It wasn't long into the reception before Vance performed as promised, stealing two minutes from his wedding duties in order to point out Molly DuVal to Josh. As if Josh hadn't been aware of the woman the moment she'd stepped out of her girly little truck. He'd been at the right place at the right time to see what she was really wearing underneath that frothy skirt she was floating around the party in, looking like a damn fairy princess.

"Be bold," Vance suggested. "She might look like refined sugar at the moment, but mention skinny-dipping and I guarantee she'll have your butt naked and in the pool before all of these guests go home."

"Really?" The thought completely intrigued Josh. "Is that something people actually do?"

Vance turned his entire body toward Josh. "What the—?" He shook his head and mumbled, "This will not do," as he pushed Josh by the scruff of his neck ahead of him. Straight toward Molly.

"Molly," Vance said without preamble. Then he leaned in and kissed her cheek. "Welcome home. Here's a little present from me to you. His name is Josh, and he just fell off the turnip truck. Now, I've got to go keep this party running smoothly, so I expect you two at the after-party around the pool. We'll catch up then."

He slapped Josh on the side of his arm and left the two of them at the bar.

"Molly, I'm Josh—"

"I know who you are, Josh McCourt," the fairy princess said right before she ordered her white wine. "We met back in high school. On the breezeway at Henderson. I showed you to the auditorium so you could give us some sort of scholarly beat down."

"I remember." Josh grinned.

"Really?" She cocked her head in an inquisitive gesture, her green eyes flashing. "I find that hard to believe."

"I'll have a beer please," Josh said to the bartender. Then to Molly, "Why would you find that hard to believe?"

She shrugged one shoulder as she picked up her drink and turned to go. "Because I did just about everything I could think of to get you to ask me out. And you didn't."

It took a moment for that to sink in. And in that moment, the fairy princess sprouted wings and flew off into the crowd. Josh wanted to leave his beer and follow her—hell, he wanted to grab her shoulder, spin her around, and get right up into her face because that was complete bullshit. Bullshit, by the way, he would have paid good money to make true.

He was finally given his beer, all fancy in a glass for God's sake, and turned, intent on searching out Miss DuVal when a large, meaty hand landed on his shoulder.

Dear God—the Father.

"Josh, my boy. A word please."

Big Jim wanted a word. During a wedding reception. At the exact moment Josh just happened to be honing in on his eldest daughter.

"I understand you're looking for some Booster funds so you can make up your fancy Google-like glasses in order to benefit the football team."

Josh blinked, dragging his mind off Molly and on to his team. "That's exactly right. I believe if I've got someone wearing them up in the press box, and I'm wearing them down on the field, I'd be able to see what's going on defensively a whole lot better. It could be a big help to decide which offense to run."

"Might be misconstrued as cheatin'."

"I like to think of it as communicating."

"Huh. Well, now—here's the deal. You might not be aware, but that lovely young lady you were just talkin' to at the bar? The one in green? She's my daughter, Molly. Now, Molly loves a good party—hell, she's just a chip off the ol' block when it comes to that. And this wedding has the makings of a great party. But she's ruffled some Henderson feathers in the past and those feathers are eyein' her up tonight. Now you—you're the sort of fellow it might do Molly some good to be seen with. Someone who has kept a low profile and won't do her reputation any harm."

"I'm not exactly sure how to take that."

"Oh, come on now. You're a good-looking kid, but you're a brainiac not a partier. I know she's probably not your type, but—just for tonight—if you could run interference from the likes of Vance Evans and his ilk, the Boosters and I'd be grateful enough to throw a little faux-Google Glass money your way."

After delivering a big smack to Josh's back, causing his beer to spill over the edge of his glass, Jim DuVal was off into the crowd.

Josh was shaking the liquid off his hand when Vance came up from behind. "Big Jim ought to learn to keep his voice down."

"You heard all that?"

"Every word. Nothin' like gettin' permission from God himself to go after the forbidden fruit." Vance grinned. "Might be a bit of a moral dilemma for a man who has kept such a low profile."

"I see no issue whatsoever."

"I don't know. Could sorta be misconstrued as cheatin'."

"Yeah. I'm going to keep thinking of it as communicating."

～∽◑∾～

"Lolly is dating Brooks Bennett?" Molly reiterated the news in astonishment. "*The* Brooks Bennett?"

"The one and only," Lucy said. "There was some big scuttlebutt surrounding Lolly, Brooks, and Vance back on the Fourth of July—you should have been around for that. But that scuttlebutt was overshadowed by the wet T-shirt contest—which, thank God, you were not here for because—" Her sister's eyes landed on Molly's chest before she rolled them, "Well, it's not like you're afraid to show them off."

"The human body—"

"Is a magnificent work of art," Lucy finished. "I know. I've heard you say so a zillion times."

"I'm just sayin' covering the body's treasures has never made any sense to me."

In her mind's eye, Molly saw images of Josh McCourt with his tuxedo shirt hanging open and his pants unzipped. Because if there were calendars made to showcase hot men with high IQs, she'd nominate Josh for the cover. There was just something about his combination of light hair and dark eyes that had struck her the moment they met. His intelligence glistened through those molasses-colored irises, creating a luscious contrast with the topaz of his hair. Looking at him made her think of that nut-covered toffee she loved to sink her teeth into and never got enough of. Pour all that into a tuxedo on a gorgeous summer evening and Molly's artistic eye was stripping him down fast. She licked her lips.

Stupid Josh.

Molly could count on one hand the number of times she was unable to flirt her way into a date. The only boy involved that she actually remembered was Josh McCourt, whom she had immediately dubbed "Hot Poindexter."

"Speaking of clothes," her sister said, interrupting her train of thought, "and before you start taking yours off, have you heard that Lolly is opening her own couture business in Henderson? The House of DuVal."

"I love the name."

"She's partnered up with Annabelle Devine to create special occasion and debutante dresses. In fact, Lolly designed that glorious concoction Aunt Genevra has on."

"Lolly? Made Aunt Gen's wedding dress?"

"I know. She's been hiding her light under a bushel, right?"

"Maybe she's just coming into her own," Molly said quietly, desperate to share just how much she'd been coming into her own lately. "Lucy, I've got some good news—"

"Why is the new assistant football coach looking at you so intently?"

"The new what?" Molly scanned the crowd, her eyes tracking right to Josh. He was about to take a sip of his beer, those sultry dark orbs calling to her from over the rim of his glass. When their gazes connected, he lowered his beer and winked.

Molly did her best not to smile.

"He's rather hunkalicious all decked out in that tux," Lucy said. *So I'm not the only one who noticed.*

Molly forced her gaze from Hot Poindexter and looked at her sister. "Josh McCourt is no football coach. Pretty sure he's some sort of computer geek."

"Yes, but now he's geeking up plays for the offense. To hear Daddy talk about it, Josh is the Second Coming."

"Really? Daddy likes him?"

"Daddy likes anyone who's going to get Henderson's football team back into the playoffs."

"So if I was seen hanging around Josh…."

"Unless you speak computerese, you'd be bored out of your mind."

"Probably," she hedged. "But if I were bored, then it would appear to all the old busybodies as if Josh McCourt had tamed me. I'd be welcomed back to Henderson sooner rather than later."

"He's from Oxford."

"I'm willing to overlook that. Once everyone sees how tame I've become, I'll quietly slip into town, start up my own House of DuVal business, and hit everyone over the head with my brilliant contributions to society before anyone knows what's happened."

"What contributions to society?"

Molly shook her head. "Haven't exactly figured that out yet."

Her sister sighed. "Molly, you're twenty-eight. You don't need anyone's permission to move back to Henderson."

"Hmm. Sort of feels like I need a lot of people's permission. Starting with Dad's and ending with Aunt Charlotte's. It's pretty obvious she still hasn't gotten over not having the chance to stuff Jacey into her old, ratty deb dress."

"You've been holding that glass of wine for a while now. Why not take a sip? Might soften your edge."

"I don't have an edge," she snapped, "and I don't like white wine."

"Then why'd you order it?"

Molly sighed. "It's a ladylike beverage and I don't want people to know I'm not drinking."

"Why in the world aren't you drinking?"

Molly gave her sister a look she hoped conveyed everything.

Lucy shook her head and tossed the word, "Boring" over her shoulder as she walked away.

CHAPTER SIX

During the past hour, Josh McCourt had been browbeaten by Brooks Bennett about not inciting members of *his* baseball team to play football. Brooks scoffed and stomped away when Josh casually mentioned he didn't realize Brooks was the head coach. Then Josh met two guys from out of town who introduced themselves as Pinks and The Outlaw. They seemed to be directing traffic at this wedding reception as much as Vance was. After that, Josh had been enchanted by an exceptional little number in a turquoise dress named Piper Beaumont until Vance came over growling and snatched her out from under his nose. He even managed to introduce himself to the bride and groom who were as gracious as they were dazzling to look at. And through it all, he continuously stole glances at Molly DuVal.

And always, always, Molly had been looking right back at him. *Hmm.*

Be bold, Vance had told him. After three weeks of unparalleled success with the football team, Josh was feeling bold.

He decided to own it.

First stop, the bar. He found a guy with the name tag *Harry* and asked a question he hoped Harry would know the answer to. "What does Molly DuVal actually like to drink?"

Harry's gaze shot over to Molly, and he smiled big, grabbing a glass and nodding his head. "Well, it sure isn't that swill she's holding on to like her life depends on it, I can tell you that. Now, I haven't actually had the pleasure of meeting that particular Miss DuVal, but from the bits and pieces I've overheard, she's bound to enjoy *this* a little bit better."

Harry handed Josh a tall glass with a pretty red-orange mixture at the bottom that bloomed into yellow by the time it got to the top. Then he splashed tequila over it. "Should do the trick," Harry said. "But be careful."

"With the woman or the drink?"

Harry smiled. "Exactly."

Josh maneuvered through the crowd but almost backtracked when he saw the circle of vultures that had formed around his fairy princess.

Bold. The word clanged loudly inside his head like a metal gong.

So he boldly stepped through the ring of fire and into the nice warm center, interrupting the conversation and taking Molly's untouched wine out of her hand. He leaned down and whispered in her ear, "White wine doesn't suit you." He placed the glass in her hand. "I'll be over by the dance floor. Waitin' on you."

Then he backed off slowly, his gaze intently holding the astonished look in her pretty green eyes.

Yeah. That got her attention.

He turned and made his way through the crowd, a bold smirk of victory pulling at his lips.

※

Yeah. That got my attention.

Molly took a sip of her pretty new drink and thought she'd let Josh McCourt cool his heels for about five minutes before she chased after him.

Or not.

Grabbing Tucker Davenport's hand, Molly pulled him through the crowd, brushing right up against Josh as she stepped onto the dance floor.

Stashing her drink might be the prudent thing to do, but she was desperately thirsty, and how much tequila could one drink hold anyway?

"Don't think I don't know what you're doin'," Tucker said. "You're just swinging me around out here trying to make Mr. Oxford jealous."

Molly countered with a brilliant smile. "Now Tucker, you know you've always been the love of my life."

"Says the town flirt."

"Just testing out the man from Oxford's mettle."

"Well, because I like to dance, I don't mind being a pawn in your little game. Now finish that drink so we can make a scene out here."

"I'm not making any scene, and I'm not guzzling down this drink," she said, moving daintily around the dance floor. "I'm sipping it. Like the lady I am."

"You're wasting a good song, is what you are." Tucker turned around and yelled, "Next!" Before Molly could protest, Tucker had swung her cousin, Vivi, into a jitterbug.

"Looks like you lost your partner." The low tone of his voice captivated her, just as it had when he'd whispered in her ear. She couldn't blame the attraction Josh was stirring up on the alcohol because she hadn't had much. And that thought made her a little suspicious.

"Why exactly did you bother bringing me this pretty drink?"

"Why were you pretending to drink wine?" he countered.

"How do you know I was pretending?"

"Because while you were watchin' me for the past hour, I was watchin' you."

His sexy grin did a good job in the fluster-me-silly department. So much so, she stammered out a lie.

"I was not watching you."

"You were," he stated as he slid his arm around her back and pulled her up against him. "Your eyes were all over me, and I can't blame you because I look damn fine in this tuxedo."

Molly's face bloomed with a reluctant smile, though she tossed out, "Now you're just being ridiculous."

"Maybe a little." His whiskey-colored eyes smiled down into hers. How he'd gotten both his arms around her, hooking his fingers together at her lower back, she'd never know. What she did know was that Hot Poindexter, with his yummy hair and eyes and those broad, broad shoulders, was making her nervous—and that was something new.

Because it was a known fact that Molly had no problem pressing her chest up against the opposite sex. But this felt different. Way different. Like she was past not-in-control and heading straight toward out-of-control. With her intention of setting a ladylike precedent, that kind of feeling would just not do. In an effort to steady herself, she pressed her free hand against his chest, pushing back to create a little more space between them.

He acquiesced, raising the side of his upper lip into a sly smile—like he knew he was knocking her off her game. "Too close for comfort?"

How was she supposed to answer that? Yes, yes, but no?

Her lashes lowered, and she gave a small shrug.

"Now don't you go getting all shy on me, Miss DuVal. I'm dancing with you because you're the kind of girl who'd sneak into the boy's locker room."

"And here I'm dancing with you hoping your low-key and studious reputation is going to help salvage mine."

"Not a chance. The words low-key and studious have been banished from my vocabulary. I'm Mr. Bold where you're concerned, and saving your reputation is definitely not my objective. It's completely up to you not to be caught somewhere you shouldn't be. However, I will do my best to restrain myself from going all statistical theory on you."

Molly laughed—and immediately noticed how good it felt. Laughing. In Henderson. Surrounded by people who knew her name. "What are you doing here?" she blurted out. "I mean, no offense, but these aren't your people."

He quirked an eyebrow. "Says the out-of-towner."

"I may live out of town," Molly grumbled, "but trust me. My heart and soul are stuck right here in Henderson."

"That should give me a fighting chance, then."

"To do what?"

"Steal your heart while you aren't lookin'."

He said it so soft, so sweet, Molly just started to melt. Right there. In his arms.

Because you're lonely, Molly reminded herself. *And apparently vulnerable.*

The last thing she needed was some wild one-night stand with Hot Poindexter. Especially now that he was the new assistant coach and creating a buzz around town. Better shut it down.

"Josh, these aren't your people."

"But they're your people. Some of them know my name. Your father knows who I am. I dare say he even likes me." Josh nodded over her shoulder. When Molly glanced back, she saw her dad giving Josh the thumbs up.

"What's that about?"

"He's under the flawed assumption that I'd be that good influence you were talkin' about."

"He put you up to this? That's why you are dancing with me?" Honest to God, her heart broke just a little bit.

"Right. Like it was your father who suggested I throw an extra shot on top of your tequila sunrise and then press my manly parts right up against your very intriguing girly parts in the middle of the damn dance floor."

"Well…." Molly stumbled, a little distracted by Hot Poindexter's manly parts—and a bit unnerved he was talking about them. "What was that thumbs up for?"

"My guess is that he wants you to move back to Henderson. I figured my manly parts would give you a good reason."

Molly stared into his eyes until she finally realized that Josh McCourt was pulling her chain. She burst out laughing.

"No?" He smiled. "Not a good enough reason? Give me a minute, and I'll think of something else."

"Josh," she said, laying a hand on his shoulder for the first time. "You've made me laugh, and I'm having fun at a big Henderson social event for the first time in a very long while. That'd be reason enough for me to want to move back. But the truth is I already want to come home. I've spent my time in exile, and I'm looking to redeem myself."

"Redeem yourself?"

"The town gossips love me. But my extended family? When I'm the subject of that gossip? Not so much. I came to this wedding planning to show Evie Jackson and her snobby followers that I deserve a place in this town. I want to show everyone that I'm not the same girl I was before."

"Yeah—no."

"What do you mean?"

"No. Absolutely not."

"I don't understand."

"Now that I've finally gotten my hands on the infamous Molly DuVal, I expect Molly DuVal—not some watered-down, boring version."

Molly sputtered. And blinked.

"Exactly. Stop with all the woe is me bullshit and show up to this party like the rock star you are."

Molly felt her mouth clap shut.

"Down the drink and put both hands on me. Pretend you're having fun."

She started to follow his orders, but once the glass was at her lips she balked. "My father's not gonna like this."

"Your father loves the rock star. He just has the unfortunate duty of being your father."

Somewhere inside of her, that statement rang true. She eyed Josh once more before downing the rest of her drink. She handed it off to a passing waiter and put a second hand on Josh's shoulders.

"Better," said Josh.

"I'm not sleeping with you."

"Yeah, ya are."

It came out so matter-of-factly, stated with such quiet certainty that it made Molly nervous. Nervous way down deep on the inside where desire and hope mingled and things got a little tingly.

She should cut her losses now, she thought. Just turn and walk away. Stick with the plan. The ladylike, play-it-safe, no-sleeping-with-Josh, really, really boring plan.

Damn! What was with all this boring talk? She wasn't boring, and she didn't have to be the life of the party to prove it. Raleigh was boring. Life without her friends and family was boring. She...

It hit her then—the truth. She couldn't come home. She, Molly DuVal—the *real* Molly DuVal, the one who preferred tequila over wine, the one who liked the way Josh's hands were sliding over her back, the one who really, really liked the nervous, tingly quiver of longing he was coaxing out—would never be able to come home.

And that hurt.

"I need another drink," she said, turning to pull Josh off the dance floor.

"No," Josh said, pulling her back into his arms. "You just need a few minutes to wrap your head around what's happening between us."

"Nothing is happening between us."

"Plenty is happening between us. And no one but you and I need to know about it."

"That's not how it works with me," she confessed. "Trust me. A nice guy like you—a teacher at the high school—you don't want your good name tangled up with mine at the end of the night."

"What are you so afraid of? Besides having a little fun? Look around you for heaven's sake." Josh turned her so that her back was up against his front. His arms crossed at her tummy, and his chin hovered just over her shoulder as he spoke. "First of all, let me remind you that this is not the Molly DuVal show. It's a wedding. If you'll notice, everyone is watching the bride and groom. Not us. Not you. And certainly not me."

Molly let her rigid stance ease a bit. Because, of course, Josh was right. The party in front of her was in full swing. Guests were either sitting down at the tables eating and drinking or crowding the bars and dance floor. She also noticed that her Aunt Genevra was making out with her groom like she was a lovestruck teenager. And that her cousin Lolly was sitting on top of a bar—*actually sitting up there*— one hand on Brooks Bennett's cheek as she leaned in to kiss him. Her own parents were on the dance floor, her mother wearing a too-tight and too-short dress to be age-appropriate, with her father's hand attached to her ass like they were in a seedy night club. She spied Lucy, Jacey, and Vivi doing shots with a cute dark-haired bartender, and the rest of her cousins were singing at the top of their lungs over there in front of the band.

Hell. She'd be the last one anybody would bother looking at right now. She turned around inside of Josh's arms and blinked up at him.

"My apple was just the first to fall off the tree, wasn't it?"

Josh cocked his head, giving her a short grin. "I've lived in this town for the last five years. The DuVal name is well respected, but it is widely known that not one of them is a wallflower. Starting with your father. You being a girl and the first of the next generation was just an unfortunate twist of fate. Now…" he shrugged, "the rest of them have joined your party."

"So it seems. But I'm still the one bad apple."

Josh shrugged. "I'm a twenty-eight-year-old brainiac who's never snuck a girl into a locker room. Wanna trade?"

Molly smiled. Josh made her smile. A lot. She leaned her cheek against his chest, not caring that the music was loud and fast.

"Your father promised me faux Google Glass if I keep you out of trouble tonight."

That had her snapping her head up. "What?"

"That happened after I had already asked Vance to introduce us."

She shook her head, not following.

"Just making sure you understand the force of nature you are up against."

"What force of nature is that exactly?"

"I'm a new man, Molly DuVal. I might have been too shy to ask you out that day back in high school, but I am now a football coach among other things, and I've developed a few fancy moves of my own. Prepare to be dazzled."

Molly burst out laughing.

"Luckily, my ego is nimble enough to dodge that reaction."

Molly's mouth hung open in an awed smile. She couldn't remember ever having someone of the opposite sex render her speechless. "I'm…flustered." She even felt herself blush when she said it. "I'm fairly certain I've never had a date make me speechless."

"Your taste in men has been less than stellar. I'm bringing more to the table. I plan to leave you speechless a lot."

Oh. My.

"You want to up your game? I'm your man. You want Henderson? I've got it in my pocket."

"Don't tell me. All I have to do is reach into your pocket, right?"

He swung her underneath his arm and then dipped her low. Leaving her defenseless in his arms and dangling inches from the floor, he said, "You, sweet Molly, don't have to do one damn thing. I'm planning to take care of all of it—but good." He swung her back up into a standing position where woozy didn't begin to describe her state.

She was sure it was that state that had her blurting, "You, Josh McCourt, are making me think about everything I shouldn't be thinking about."

To which he calmly stated, "Now we're finally getting somewhere."

CHAPTER SEVEN

True to his word, Hot Poindexter, a.k.a Josh McCourt, took Molly by the hand and showed her that he did indeed have Henderson in his pocket. The boy from Oxford, Henderson's rival town, stole a glass of champagne off a passing waiter's tray, whispered in the man's ear, and then dragged Molly behind him right over to none other than Evie Jackson.

"Mrs. Jackson," Josh said, interrupting the conversation at her table.

Molly, horrified as she scanned the upturned faces one by one, realized she could name each one of the old biddies sitting there sporting their silver-grey updos and ancient pearls. This was bigger than just Evie Jackson. Josh had brought her right to the nucleus of Henderson's society. To the foot of the formidable mountain she had to climb. This was the generation most unlikely to forgive her. This was the generation she had to persuade to ease their harsh assessment.

And here she was…speechless.

"I'm sorry to interrupt, but I wanted to bring you this champagne as a thank you for that kind note you sent me," Josh was saying. The waiter arrived then with a tray full of champagne glasses. "And I didn't want to leave out these other young ladies," Josh said as the women clapped hands and tittered as champagne was placed before them. "I am happy to hear the Garden Club was able to make use of the vegetable software. I took a walk over to the plot of land you ladies have transformed so beautifully and noticed you've got quite the bumper crop going this year. I confess the tomatoes were in such abundance I took a couple home with me."

"Oh, Josh." Evie Jackson swatted at him flirtatiously. "You take what you want from that garden. I mean it. Our thumbs would not be nearly so green if it wasn't for your soil tests and computer-generated layouts."

"Ladies, I believe y'all know my date, and the bride's niece, Molly DuVal."

Date?

"Hmm," Evie said, giving Molly careful scrutiny. "Molly."

"Mrs. Jackson," Molly said meekly.

Josh dove right in. "I understand Molly was engaged to your grandson, Mrs. Jackson."

What the hell?

"Mmm. Yes. Breakin' her engagement to our Tyler is probably what Molly is best known for around here," Evie said, caging her harsh remark with her full-on Southern belle smile. "A word to the wise, Josh."

"How is Tyler doing these days?" Josh proceeded undaunted.

Mrs. Jackson's smile became genuine. "Why he's just had twins," she whispered—completely in awe. "Two beautiful baby girls. Named after me and his other grandmother."

"I bet you could not be prouder." Josh beamed back at her.

"No, I honestly could not," Evie agreed.

Josh dropped his voice just a bit. "So, it worked out for the best then."

"It did," Evie agreed. As those words sunk in—Molly saw it happen—Evie's expression changed, and she looked back over at Molly and nodded.

It was subtle. But the change was there.

Josh.

"And how 'bout your son's boy, Mrs. Z? And his buddy, Mrs. Simms' grandson and yours too, Mrs. Swift? That little scuttle out by the lake get itself all worked out?"

Mrs. Zimmerman and the other ladies laughed nervously. "Oh, Josh…you know…boys will be boys."

"And girls will be girls," he said bringing Molly in closer with his right arm around her waist. "Mrs. Egan, I understand that you were quite the scandalous debutante back in your day. How many times were you engaged before Mr. Egan managed to wrestle you down the aisle?"

Dottie Egan blushed proudly.

"Henderson has a rich history, starting right here with all of you beautiful women. I'm doing my best to convince Molly to leave all the glories of Raleigh and come home. Take her rightful place in the heart of Henderson's history and continue the grand traditions that your mothers started and y'all continue to uphold today.

"Oh, Molly," Mrs. Egan said. "You *should* come home. This town is dryin' up faster than my skin in winter with all you youngsters leavin' for greener pastures. We need the young people to stick around and start raising families again. Keep this town viable. Isn't that right, Evie? You said so yourself when Tyler moved away."

Evie Jackson turned her full attention to Molly. She even reached out and took her by the hand. "It's true, Molly. I'm afraid it's going to be left to your generation to turn this town around. We need girls like you to come back home and raise families here."

"Girls like me?" Molly choked out.

"Exactly like you," Evie Jackson assured her with a tug to her hand. "Girls who are movers and shakers and won't be afraid to get things done around here. Now enough of all this. You two get out there and dance. Us old women need something to talk about, so git."

As Josh clasped Molly's hand and pulled her away, she whispered, "We are staying off the dance floor. I refuse to give them one more thing to talk about."

"Fine," Josh agreed as they approached the bar. "Because you and I have a few things that need settling." .

"I'm still not sleeping with you."

"Oh." Josh pulled her around to face him and grinned wickedly. "You think I did all that just so I could get in your pants?"

"Well, didn't you?"

"No. I did that so you'd stop worrying about changing your stripes. I did that so the real Molly DuVal—the rock star—can finally move back home. I did that so that I can *then* initiate my very tricked-out plan of seduction to get in your pants."

"Tricked-out plan of seduction?"

"I've got an app for that."

Hot Poindexter didn't need an app. He was doing just fine on his own. Making her feel a little giddy and lulling her into a false sense of security that she was going to be allowed back through the gates of Henderson.

"Well, thank you for that. With Evie," she added as Josh ordered them drinks. "You accomplished in a few minutes what I had figured would take me months of well-placed, well-timed, serene social outings."

"Yeah—no. I don't have time for that. We are fast trackin' you back to Henderson. So what's next?"

"Well, if you can work your magic and dazzle Aunt Charlotte over there into forgiving me for getting Jacey left off the debutante list, it'd be smooth sailing."

"All right then. Come on."

Molly stumbled along behind him, her hand firmly in Josh's grasp. He stood her right next to Aunt Charlotte and her two best friends who were in the middle of howling about one funny thing or another—all of them on the brink of slurring their words.

"Molly!" Aunt Charlotte looked a little startled, like she wasn't certain whether she'd just been overheard.

Molly was plenty startled herself. She felt a push from behind and heard Josh's quiet command in her ear. "Fast track. Improvise."

"Aunt Charlotte," Molly said breathlessly. "Miss Mary, Miss Caroline." Molly nodded in greeting to the other two ladies.

"It's good to see you here, Molly," Miss Mary said kindly.

"Thank you. Thank you for that. Because it's good to be back," Molly said, twisting her hands together. "I've missed Henderson. Missed the family and missed my friends. Raleigh has a lot to offer, but you know—you need your people." She bobbed her head, anxious.

"That's true," Miss Caroline agreed. "Why, the three of us have known each other since we had our babies together." She indicated her good friends standing in the circle. "I don't know what I'd do if one of you decided to move away."

"Oh—don't even think of it," Aunt Charlotte said. "Havin' your friends close by—well, that's just everything, isn't it?"

"It is," Molly agreed. "I can tell you from experience that new friends are wonderful and can certainly broaden your horizons. But, old friends and cousins," she said, looking at her Aunt Charlotte, "well, there's no replacing those."

Aunt Charlotte put her arm around Molly. "You want to come home."

"I do. I'm planning to move back."

"Well, I'll tell you, your cousins will be very happy to hear this news."

Molly struggled to pull her courage together, knowing that if she didn't address the elephant in the room now, she never would.

"What about you, Aunt Charlotte?" she ventured sincerely. "I've been racking my brain for ways to make up the lack of Jacey's debut to you—and frankly, the only thing I can think of is to ask my friend, David, a portrait photographer, to take some shots of Jacey in your deb dress. It would be my treat. He's a gifted artist, and it might be fun for Jacey to haul your dress to Raleigh for a sitting. I could arrange for a makeup artist to do her face and a stylist to do her hair. I know it would never replace the ball, but maybe having a framed picture of Jacey in your gown sitting next to your own debutante portrait in the living room might make the disappointment a little more tolerable."

"That is a wonderful idea," Miss Mary squealed. "Jessie-belle and I'll join you. Remember, she was going through that God-awful black-hair phase when she came out? The pictures are atrocious. I would love to have a portrait done now that she's back to her natural color."

"Sure," Molly said. "We'll make a day of it. Throw in a little shopping and lunch."

"Molly, that is very thoughtful. And generous," her aunt said quietly, looking truly touched. "I can't think of anything I'd like more."

"Good."

Standing under her aunt's forgiving gaze, Molly felt her shoulders let go of long-held tension. She might not sleep with Hot Poindexter tonight, but she was definitely going to kiss him. She hugged her aunt and then introduced Josh as her date.

They walked away from the ladies hand in hand, strolling out of the tent where the evening was stretching out, showing off its last gasps of light in a glorious display. The day's weather had been spectacular and the night ahead promised as much. Molly let her mind float, taking in the gentle breeze, the rolling hills, and an unparalleled feeling of contentment.

Josh had done that for her. Who knew Hot Poindexter was a take-charge, grab-the-bull-by-the-horns kind of guy? Wasn't that generally her role?

They stood together, away from the crowds, facing the sunset. "So…," she finally asked, feeling like she indeed owed him something, "what is it you want from me, Josh?"

Josh chuckled. "I have not minced words, darlin'."

She turned her face toward his, quirking a brow.

"Move home. We'll figure the rest out."

She looked back toward the sunset. After a while, she told the truth as she saw it. "I'm not smart enough for you."

She felt his thumb rub over hers. "I'm smart enough for the both of us."

She laughed.

The moment quieted and she confessed more. "I'm not planning on coming home and tearing it up, but you've seen the rest of the DuVals in action. I'm probably still gonna be a handful."

"Then it's a good thing I've got two."

She had to give him credit. The man sure knew how to make her smile.

Finally, Molly turned to Josh, sighing. "What's really going on here?"

He shook his head. "I'm lonely," he said, granting her a little smile. "Simple as that. I've led a fairly solitary life following my intellectual pursuits. Now I'm an assistant coach and I see all these young guys, old guys too, having fun. Being a part of something. A team. A crowd. A group of friends. A community. I want that. I want to be a part of something."

"Not sure how I fit in, exactly."

He shrugged. "I caught my front line chasing girls around the locker room. Looked like fun. One of the girls was your cousin, Tinley. She looks a lot like you did back then. Made me think of the time we met. How pretty you were. How you flirted with me even though I was nothin'. But what I especially remember was your kindness. How you went out of your way to save me from further embarrassment. How you walked with me, showing me the way to the auditorium—talkin' with me the whole time like I was important—and then, wishin' me luck.

"I'm sure that's how you treated everybody. Probably still do. But that's not how most people operate. I know that for sure. So to be exposed to that sort of kindness, especially during high school—when not a lot of that was going around—meant something. That day we met, I became a Molly DuVal fan."

Molly knew her heart was beating, because she could hear it echoing loudly in her ears. Felt all of her pulse points pounding. But she wasn't breathing. No air in and no air out. Just the lone heartbeat as she digested his gentle words. Most guys liked her because she was a party girl and wasn't afraid to get naked. No one, except her father, had ever commented on her kindness.

"I didn't have the courage to sneak a pretty girl into the locker room back then," Josh continued. "But I do now. So I started thinkin' maybe I could convince the infamous Molly DuVal to let me chase her around a bit."

She laughed, grateful for his segue. Hoping to cover the bit of emotion she was trying to choke down. She lightened it up further by saying, "What's in it for me, exactly?"

Josh spread his arms wide and gave her an expression of disbelief. "Come on. Now that Hale Evans is off the market, I've got to be the—what?—twenty-third most eligible bachelor in Henderson."

Molly felt herself beam watching his antics. Felt like she was glowing from the inside out. Hot Poindexter had it all going on, and from his expression, he knew it too.

Hmm.

Molly started taking the pins out of her hair. Letting her French twist fall into wavy curls down her back.

She saw a stricken look cross over Josh's face. "What the hell are you doing?"

"Letting my hair down."

"I see that," Josh said as he moved in closer. "Why now? Why here?"

Molly shrugged and grabbed his hand, leading him back toward the tent and the party that was starting to rock hard. "It's a metaphor. One a smart guy like you ought to appreciate. Figured it was time for Molly DuVal the Rock Star to show up at her aunt's wedding."

"Oh, Lord."

Molly stopped short. "What?" she asked, laughing at his pained expression. "You've been telling me all night you didn't want any watered-down version."

"True. But now—with your hair down, and you being…you again—I am bound to be faced with some stiff competition."

"Now, what could you possibly be worried about?" She smiled, moving in to peck his lips. "After all, you're the twenty-third most eligible bachelor in Henderson."

CHAPTER EIGHT

Josh couldn't say for sure whether Molly DuVal, Rock Star, actually showed up, since he'd never had the pleasure to see her in action. But the girl who danced, drank, and sang the night away with him was definitely rockin' his world.

Taking her hair down was one thing—all kinds of shades of blond—it made his fingers twitchy wanting to grab hold of it and twirl her around. Then once Genevra and Hale left for their honeymoon, Molly kicked off her green high heels, making herself a full head shorter than him. Making her seem a little more real, a little more approachable. He liked that. A lot. And once the band quit, most of the guests began to head home, but Pinks and The Outlaw took over the stage with drums and a guitar, starting up the after-party. During that jam session, Molly's tulle skirt went flying, and now she danced around him in what could barely be called a dress. He took to calling her Lady Godiva because her hair was practically as long as her hemline.

His worry over competition for her attention was short lived. She turned down all comers, and there were plenty. She focused her attention on him completely—unless her cousins were dancing together to some silly song they all needed to scream at the top of their lungs. That's when he'd leave the dance floor to search out a couple bottles of ice-cold water.

Because they both drove.

And having Molly wind up incarcerated would put a real glitch in his plans to get her back in Henderson for good.

The night wore on. The caterers cleaned up and left. One lone bartender, Harry, in fact, stayed to take care of the fifty or so friends and family who wouldn't let it end. Josh looked around but couldn't find Vance to thank him for the invitation. So he went to sit next to one tired-looking Brooks Bennett while Molly circled up with the rest of the crazy DuVals and hangers-on on the dance floor. He handed Brooks a bottle of water, and the man seemed grateful for it.

"So," Brooks said. "You got a thing for Molly?"

"Molly? Hmm, now which one is she?"

"Save it. It's plain embarrassing the way you've been panting on her heels all night."

"Says the guy who looks like he wanted to leave hours ago."

"Touché." They clinked water bottles.

"I do," Josh admitted. "I have a thing for Molly. I want her to move back to Henderson."

"You are preaching to the choir," Brooks said as he opened the bottle and took a sip. "It's starting to feel like my life's mission is to get people to move back to Henderson."

"How can I help?"

"Says the man from Oxford."

"Oxford's not going anywhere. I work here. I want the town to thrive."

Brooks looked him over, skeptical. Then his face changed, completely. Finally, he leaned in and said, "Can you keep a secret?"

"Sure."

"No "sure." I'm asking you man to man. Can you keep a secret? Because this town has a problem with that sort of thing."

"I'm from Oxford."

"Well, all right then," Brooks said, coming alive as he spoke. "Vance Evans and I have formed a team. A team with the sole purpose of brainstorming, researching, evaluating, and then implementing ways to bring more economic prosperity to this town. We've got a big idea brewing, but to pull it off, Henderson is probably going to need some Oxford land. Now, it could certainly benefit both towns and the surrounding areas. But Lord knows anything new and innovative, not to mention anything that requires working hand in hand with Oxford, is going to be a hard sell around here. Maybe if you were a part of the team you could shed some insight into the mindset of the key players over there. Help us think through the pros and cons of what we're trying to do. You're known to have a hell of a brain and mean computer skills. Hell, if you can make our football team look good, I'm sure there'd be plenty you could help us with."

"I'm in."

"You're in? Just like that? No questions at all?"

"I have discovered I really like being part of a team. And it just so happens to be paying dividends tonight. You got a team—I want to be on it. I'll do my best to contribute."

"That's great," Brooks said before he was barreled into by a cute, young brunette. He threw his arms around her and regained his balance like the athlete he was. He kissed her quick and turned her around to introduce her to Josh.

"Nice to meet you, Lolly," Josh said.

Lolly was breathing hard, glistening with sweat, and smiling big. She pulled some hair from her cheek and nodded. "Bring Molly to the pool. A few of us are sticking around for a late night swim."

Josh bit back a laugh as Brooks shook his head and mouthed the words, "No…we're…not," over Lolly's head.

"Thanks for the invite," he said, smiling at Lolly. Then he stood up, spying Molly standing off to the side, watching him. He held out his hand, and she moved forward to take it.

That made him feel tall. Real tall.

They started walking toward her shoes, her skirt, her purse, and God only knew what else as the crowd around them hugged and said their good-byes. He was trying to figure out how this night was going to end when a hand landed on his shoulder.

Big Jim DuVal spun him around and held out his hand, saying good night. He looked over at his daughter and gave her a happy smile. "Two o'clock is a little late to be driving all the way back to Raleigh. How 'bout you sleep in your old room tonight? Stay and have some breakfast with the family tomorrow. Talk a few things out."

"I'd like that," Molly said. Then father and daughter hugged, and Josh could see that Molly fought to choke back some emotion.

They pulled apart, and Big Jim nodded to both of them before heading off to collect his wife. Molly gave her mom a little wave from afar before turning her full attention on him.

"You moving back?"

"I believe I am," she said, twisting right and left like a happy little girl.

"I'm glad," he told her.

She wrapped the fairy princess skirt around her waist and fastened it. But she dangled her shoes from her fingers, along with her purse.

"Walk you to your car?"

"I'd like that," she said.

The two of them crowded onto one of the last few golf carts, where Josh had the opportunity to meet her sisters Lucy and Lilly along with their dates.

No valets waited, but all cars and keys were accounted for, lined up in the Evans' circular drive and on out toward the gate. The DuVal clan dispersed quickly, allowing Josh to forgo a trumped-up excuse to get Molly to linger with him. He wanted a few minutes alone.

They slowly walked, hand in hand toward her little truck. As they got close, it was obvious the thing hadn't been washed in ages. He wondered if she'd mock his spotless Prius, now the lone car waiting off in the distance.

"So," he said as they reached her door.

"So," she repeated, turning to face him. Her smile was so big it made him smile right back at her.

He cleared his throat, taking up her other hand and raising both as he entwined their fingers, pressing palm against palm. "Molly, Molly, Molly." He really did not want to let her go. "Tonight certainly ranks up there as one of the fastest nights of my life. It flew by. I don't feel like I've had enough time with you. So, in case I haven't made myself perfectly clear, I'd like to see you again."

"Sounds like you're declaring the evening over."

"I think you know I'd like nothing better than to string it out, but seeing as your father is waitin' on you to come home—"

"My father stopped waiting on me to come home a long time ago. Probably before he should have, poor man."

There was his opening. And he was a smart man. Smart enough to know that when the woman whose hair you wanted to get all tangled up in gives you an opening, you walk through it—without hesitation.

So he stepped in and closed the distance between them, wrapping his hands in her hair. His face directly over hers, his focus solely on her lips. He didn't know where the words came from, they just came out, quiet and rough.

"Then here's how it's going to work," he told her. "I'll hold on to your keys and your car stays here. When we get to my place, I'm in charge. Rumor has it you may be pretty quick at shedding your clothes, but tonight your clothes stay on until I take them off. You and I are taking it slow. I'll get you to your parents before first light and make sure your car is in their driveway by the time you want to head back to Raleigh."

"One question."

"Yeah—no. No questions." He leaned in and kissed her lips, but like she'd done to him earlier, it was just a quick peck. Their first real kiss was yet to come.

"Anything you need out of your car?"

"There's a bag. In the back. And my flip-flops." He took the bag while she dropped her flip-flops to the ground and stepped into them, leaving her heels in the truck.

"Keys."

She reached in, pulled them from the ignition, and handed them to him.

"Ready?"

She nodded. He took her hand and off they went.

"You're doing it again," he heard her mumble.

"Doing what?" he asked, dragging her along.

"Making me nervous."

He stopped dead. "I? Make *you*, nervous?"

She shrugged her shoulders together in a gesture that made her look small, cute, and vulnerable.

"I'm okay with that," he decided, pulling her along to his car. He swung the passenger door open and seated her inside.

Once he got in, he started the car up and turned the radio down. If he stopped to think about what was going on, he'd be scared to death. The fact that he made Molly DuVal nervous evened the playing field.

He put the car in drive, reached over, and took her hand, holding on to it all the way home.

~⁓~

The tiny house Josh rented was stacked with books, CDs, games, game systems, laptops, monitors, computers, and computer parts. Molly took in the lone leather La-Z-Boy chair in front of the huge flat screen TV and said, "I take it you don't entertain much."

"Nope. And standing here looking at it through your eyes, I now see why. Probably need a couch. Maybe some bookshelves to store all this crap. Hard to believe I'm lonely when my place looks like this," he joked.

Molly wandered toward the kitchen. "Trust me. Owning a couch and some bookshelves doesn't ward off loneliness."

"Don't tell me a rock-star party girl like you gets lonely," he teased, coming up behind her.

"Desperately," she breathed.

She felt Josh smooth a hand down the back of her head. It soothed her as much as it heightened her awareness of him. She felt his warmth behind her and closed her eyes as he whispered in her ear. "That's why we're fast tracking you back to Henderson. Back to your people. Your lonely days are over."

She let her neck fall to the side as Josh's fingers combed her hair back off her shoulder. When she felt his lips drift along the side of her throat, she tried to remember if she'd ever been kissed like this. Simply. Slowly. Delicately. She relaxed into the moment. He had said he wanted to take charge, and if this was how he intended to do it, she was going to relish it.

She licked her lips. "What about you?" she asked quietly. "What about your lonely days?"

She felt his hand fist in her hair as he turned her face toward him. "I'm working on it," he said, right before his lips captured hers. She smiled, parting her lips, and he took advantage by sliding his tongue in between. That first intimate touch—his tongue on hers—

made her body sigh. Heat tingled up her cheeks and crept down her chest. She felt his hands pull her around, pressing her up against him in a way that was so much better than they'd managed on the dance floor. His hand splayed wide and possessively against the center of her back. She liked the feel of that. The feel of what it conveyed.

She reached up and wrapped her arms around his neck, enjoying the slow, languid way he kissed. Like every tantalizing touch counted. Like he was coaxing her along, not rushing anything. Her body responded by letting go of tension, sinking into his torso ever so slightly, allowing his possession to grow. A contented hum slipped out, unbidden, as her mind started to tune itself down, drifting into a state of pleasure.

Josh's fingers started with a gentle touch at her temple and then combed back through her hair. So sweet, so easy, that tingles drifted after them. She pulled back slightly, a dazed smile on her lips. She drank in those luscious dark-colored eyes, seeing a seriousness that hadn't been there before.

"I'd like to take this into the bedroom," he whispered. She gave a brief nod and bit her lip, dropping her gaze to the floor as he took her by the hand and led her down the hallway.

The giddiness just bubbled up out of nowhere. She tried to suppress it, but by the time she was standing before his bed, she couldn't help but giggle. Hot Poindexter. After all these years.

"What?" Josh asked, sending his own little laugh back at her.

"Can you believe we are doing this? You and I?"

"If you are asking if I can believe that I've got Molly DuVal standing in my bedroom, then no. No, that I cannot believe."

"Oh, I'm not just standing in your bedroom. I'm about to take off my clothes."

"No. No, no, no. *I'm* about to take off your clothes."

Whatever. Antsy just to have them off, Molly spun, twisting the length of her hair into a bun and holding it high so that Josh had access to the zipper of her dress. But that wasn't where the next sensation came. No. She felt his fingertips at both sides of the curve of her waist, resting there. Waiting. She felt them begin to tickle, begin to move, slowly trailing back and forth along the edge of her satin belt. A soft kiss landed on the exposed skin of her neck, sending tingles down from there to the points where his fingertips lingered. Those fingertips were a luxurious treat she hadn't expected. Even through the fabric of her dress, her body relished his touch. So focused on the divine sensations, she hardly noticed when her tulle skirt disappeared.

The rich warmth of his voice rumbled gently against her ear. "I liked watching you flit around the wedding in all this puffy stuff. Made you look like a grown-up fairy princess. I kept expecting to see wings, because it certainly took me all night to capture you." He nuzzled into her neck then, tickling her as he did. The skirt may have vanished, but his fingertips were back at her sides, moving in lazy circles at her waist.

His touch, she was discovering, was a unique and precious thing. Slow and easy. Sensuous even in its light playfulness. All of her focus moved to the sensations being created by his fingertips as they drifted slowly up and down her sides, feeling every tantalizing touch through the sheer fabric of her dress.

"You know the male mind can run itself off on some peculiar tangents," he whispered as he caressed her. "All night, I just kept wondering, 'If she's wearing emerald from head to toe, what color is she wearing underneath?'"

Those fingertips made a lazy sweep across her back and finally up to the top of her spine. Keeping true to form, they dazzled even as they maneuvered the zipper slowly down her back. His lips added to her pleasure by trailing after his light touch, placing soft, slow, kisses on her flesh as it was exposed.

Her head fell forward as she reveled in his touch. For the first time ever, she was not in a race to get rid of her clothes. For the first time ever, wearing clothes just so they could be taken off—like this, with such poignant grace, such intense focus—made sense.

Josh.

His fingertips led his palms as they flattened across her shoulder blades and drifted into the space between skin and fabric. He pushed the dress from her shoulders and down her arms, leaving her exposed from the waist up, except for her pretty lace bra, which was not emerald green.

She actually heard Josh swallow.

It made her smile.

Pretty much everything Josh did made her smile.

She felt those magic fingertips draw a lazy path down to her hips, where he managed to scoot his hands inside her dress, linger over her hips, and slide the fabric south enough where it then fell to the floor. Molly turned her head to the side to look at Josh behind her, and caught him staring at her ass.

"Nude?" he exclaimed in shock. "All night long, you were nude under the dress?"

"I wasn't nude," she insisted, turning around to face him. She held her arms out wide to prove it.

Josh sputtered, "Well, well…this," he said, throwing out a hand toward her torso, "is practically the same thing. I was expecting emerald green. Or red. Or bright pink."

Molly looked down at her matching lace lingerie. Yes, it could be considered nude in color, and it did sort of blend in with her skin tone, but she thought it was pretty. "You don't like it?"

"On the contrary," Josh said, reaching down to pick up her tulle skirt. "I like it very much. I like it a lot better than red, or green, or anything—anything at all that I could imagine. Only, now…."

"Now what?"

"Now, I want to see what you look like in nothing but your fairy princess skirt and…." He flashed his hand in front of her chest and hips. "Whatever you call that. May I?" He stepped forward and drew the skirt back around her naked waist, fumbling a bit with the catch on the bow, but as long as his fingertips were fussing over her flesh, Molly was content to let him handle it.

"There," he said, stepping back and appraising. His mouth hung open, his dreamy eyes explored up and down her body. For a woman who had no problem standing naked for hours as an artist's model, she suddenly felt overexposed. In an effort to "do something" and to extend Josh's obvious appreciation, she began a slow twirl in front of him. Taking time to smooth the layers of tulle that had wrinkled, fluffing out the pretty green skirt, coming around to owning her femininity in a way she never had before.

As she came full circle, her heart opened and embraced the man who stood dumbfounded in front of her.

"You are exquisite," he whispered. "There is not another word for it," he said as his gaze moved to her face, to her eyes, as he smiled an I'm-not-quite-believing-what-is-happening smile. "Molly DuVal."

"In the flesh."

He started to take off his jacket. She came forward and began to untie his bow tie, but let it lay undone around his neck as she started with the top stud of his shirt. "Can I get you to show me one thing before we take all this off?"

"A condom?" he asked in all seriousness.

"No," she laughed. "But that's good too." Her hands went back to work opening up his shirt. "It's just that while you were picturing me in my underwear, I was picturing you...sort of...like this." She finished by unzipping his pants in one fast move and then standing back.

"Here," she said, grabbing up his jacket. "Hold this like a model would. Over your shoulder. Right, right—now put your other hand in the pocket of your pants. Perfect," she said, her gaze rolling over him, assessing him from head to toe with an artistic eye. She made a few tweaks to his shirt, turned his head to the side a bit and then stood back and took him in.

"And there you are. Hot Poindexter. Cover model for IQ Weekly."

"Hot what?" he exclaimed.

"My pet name for you in high school," she said, still taken in by the whole of the man in front of her. "Because you were hot...and, you know...crazy smart."

"Can I move now?"

"Ahhh—" Molly let her eyes rove over him one last time before saying, "Sure."

"Good." Josh dropped his jacket, tore off his shirt, and had Molly dumped on the bed behind her before she knew what was happening.

"Poindexter," he mumbled in discontent as he kicked off his pants.

Molly shrieked and rolled to the center of the bed, covering her eyes as Josh made to leap on it and her. A hand grabbed her shoulder, rolling her flat on to her back. She was caged in by his arms and it thrilled her. Completely.

"Back to me being in charge," he said. "There will be no wrestling with me for the top."

"What if I like the top?" she said, licking her lips.

"That would not come as a surprise to me," he said, leaning down and getting his lips tangled up with hers. "I'm just willing," he said as they kissed, laying his body slowly against hers, "to work real hard," he said as his hands went underneath her to unhook her bra, "at changing your mind."

She raised her arms as he slid the lace off. "Not much to all this now is there?" he said, studying her bra a moment before he tossed it away. "Where were we?" he teased. But when his gaze traveled down to her chest, his expression grew taut and serious.

"Molly," he breathed as he looked his fill. "Molly. You steal my breath." He let his body tip to the side, his arm bending, bringing up a hand to support his head. Then his other arm came up, letting his fingertips trail over what his eyes beheld.

They trailed across the upper curves of her breasts, delicately, as if they were gliding over precious silk. She watched his earnest expression as he noticed goosebumps form under his touch. Had a man ever looked at her like this before? Been so enthralled? Had a man ever taken the time to *study* her as Josh was doing? His thumb came from below and then his hand flattened underneath her breast and slid up, his open palm swirling over her peaked nipple. She closed her eyes, relishing his attention.

His lips pressed against hers, opening her up to a soul-stirring kiss before he pulled away and began using his mouth to tantalize the rest of her body. He told her he was going to take his time, as his tongue worked its magic on her breasts. He told her he was going to be taking her apart, as he unfastened her skirt with his teeth. He promised he would put her back together again after he was done, as he slid her lace undies down to her knees. A possessive hand spread one knee to the side, leaving her foot trapped against her other knee and bound by her panties.

She stroked her nails over his scalp, through his short butterscotch locks as those talented fingertips toyed their way slowly along her damp, needy center. And true to his word, when his mouth went to work, he took her apart, bit by teeny…tiny…bit.

CHAPTER NINE

"Come on, Princess," Josh whispered against her cheek. "I promised I'd have you to your daddy's by first light."

Molly groaned into the mattress.

"Come on. We're runnin' out of moonlight here."

"I don't care," she croaked. "You promised you'd put me back together, and I am about as undone as I can be."

There was no doubting the damn man had an app for that. He had an arsenal full of tricks, and over the past three hours he'd shown off every one of them. Tricks to keep her off kilter, tricks to make her feel things she'd never felt before, tricks that allowed him to take his damn time once he finally, finally pushed all that magnificent length inside of her. He had her begging for more right before she pleaded for release. And what a release it was. She smiled at the memory. She'd never felt so complete. So spent. So enamored. All she'd wanted to do was curl up into his arms and hold on to Josh. But those crazy fingertips of his continued to work their magic and within a matter of minutes he'd gotten her riled up and eager for more.

Of course, that's when she broke the rules by scrambling on top of his long body. But after all his earlier efforts, he seemed happy to lie back and watch her go.

"Come on." He slapped her bare tushy to get her moving. "We do not want our little dalliance to end up being the lead story at all the hot gossip spots. The faster we get you moved back to Henderson, the faster I can manhandle you back into my bed."

She smiled, rolling over onto her back and stretching luxuriously, loving the idea of coming back to this bed. "I look forward to being manhandled."

She heard him mumble, "Give me strength," before he started throwing her clothes at her. "If I wasn't already dressed, I swear your daddy would be painting his gun white in about five months. Princess, I am fresh out of condoms, so if you don't have an interest in a shotgun wedding, you'd best be gettin' yourself dressed. Fast."

She would. She'd make it home before first light because that was what her Hot Poindexter wanted. But first, she knelt on the bed and captured him with her arms and lips.

"Just in case I have to make a quick exit," she said as she kissed him, "I want you to know…."

When the kiss dragged on, Josh finally pulled away and said, "What? You want me to know…what?"

He must have seen it then. Everything she couldn't find the words to convey was surely there, banked within the emotion drowning her eyes.

"So much for best laid plans," he said, then mumbled something about the human factor as he took her mouth in his patent soul-stirring kiss and laid her down.

It was past noon, and just as church was letting out, when the two of them strolled hand-in-hand up big Jim's drive, wearing exactly what they'd had on the night before.

Thanks for reading *Taming Molly*. If you're curious about Hale and Genevra whose wedding you just attended, and Lolly, Brooks, and Vance's love triangle check out my full length novels:

Good Cop
Heroes of Henderson ~ Book 1

Bad Cop
Heroes of Henderson ~ Book 2

If you want more of Molly and Josh and want to know what the gift was in the pizza box, check out:

Top Dog
Heroes of Henderson ~ Book 3

Crain Carraway, Dallas business tycoon and sports fanatic, is not from Henderson. But his wife is. Although no one knows that because she managed to get cold feet *after* their impromptu Vegas wedding. Hiding out in her hometown, she's sicced her daddy's lawyers on him, doing her best to buy his silence and a quickie divorce.

Like hell.

It's taken him way too long to find the perfect Mrs. Carraway, and now that he's had the fortuitous luck to stumble into Henderson and his bride, he's not about to let her go.

Read on for a sneak peek.

CHAPTER ONE

The trouble with trouble is it always starts out as fun.

Four Months Earlier

Crain Carraway slipped inside the luxurious bathroom of his Las Vegas suite and shut the door quietly. Even though he couldn't sleep, it seemed that his beautiful bride was out cold after a very lengthy, highly energetic, totally off-the-charts, roll-me-over-and-do-that-again consummation of their marriage. God, she was something. Something fine looking and brilliant and just as sweet as the cherry on top of his Absolut Old Fashioned. He couldn't believe she was his. All his. And he couldn't sleep because he wanted the world to know it.

Starting with his parents.

He dialed their number, checking the time on his watch. Dallas was two hours ahead of Vegas and on a weekday morning his parents should be up and at 'em. No doubt this would get their day started with a bang.

"Honey Bear!" his momma said in greeting, as if he wasn't thirty-five-years old.

"Momma Bear," he said back, playing her game. "Put me on speaker and round up Poppa Bear. I have big news."

"Big news?"

"Texas-sized news."

His mother laughed. "Bigger than when you started CC Dallas, Inc.? Lucius!" his mother shouted. "Your son has Texas-sized news he wants us to hear together."

"May as well grab a bottle of champagne while you're at it, Ma. You're gonna need it." Crain said.

"I'll bet that luxury suite at Cowboys Stadium came through," his father's voice echoed over the phone.

"Even better than that," Crain said, grinning at himself in the bathroom mirror. "Dad, do you remember that statuesque blonde I pointed out when you stopped in the office a month ago? The one trying to hide all that beauty under those smart-girl glasses?"

"Do I? That pretty little gal had you drooling like a Bluetick Coonhound."

Crain chuckled. "Guilty as charged. Well, it took some doing, but I finally got that pretty little gal to agree to a dinner date. I took her to Nick & Sam's."

"Best steakhouse in Dallas," his dad said.

"And she loved it. In fact, the date went so well she agreed to meet me for drinks at the Ice House the next night. One thing led to another very good night and, although I will admit she was a little bit tipsy when I asked her to accompany me to Las Vegas, I assure you she was completely sober when I asked her to marry me."

"You're engaged?" his mother exclaimed.

"Better than that. We're married."

"Married?" Poppa Bear sounded astonished.

"We eloped. Just last night. It was just…right. Everything about it was perfect. And I'm sorry you weren't here, but I know you're gonna forgive me when you meet my bride."

"Wha…ah…well of course we'll forgive you," his mother stuttered. "But darlin' boy, this is all so quick. So sudden."

Crain smiled, softening his voice in an effort to soothe his momma. "I know it seems that way, I truly do. But you know I've dated a lot of wonderful women over the years. Every time I figured out what I didn't want, I knew better what I did want. And this one, this one is the complete package. Underneath her bright and engaging business persona, there's a bewitching temptress just as sweet as praline pie. She's the one I've been looking for all my life, Momma. She's the one I want."

"You sound so certain."

"Because I am. I was certain the first time we met, and after date number two all I could think was how fast can I get this girl to the altar?"

"Any faster and you'd catch up to yesterday," his father said.

"And now I'm burning daylight, so let me get back to my bride," Crain countered.

"Wait!" his mother cried. "What's her name? Who are her people?"

"Well, I don't exactly know who her people are, Momma, because I've been solely focused on sweeping her off her feet. But I'll tell you what. Anybody who can raise a woman like her can't be all bad. Now I've got to go and talk my bride into a nice long honeymoon in Hawaii, so if you two don't hear from me for a couple weeks, don't fret. In the meantime, Momma, you can start planning whatever extravaganza you've got in mind to introduce my bride to *our* people."

"I can tell you one thing," his momma scolded. "It's gonna look a whole lot like a church wedding and a big fat reception. You tell my new daughter-in-law the first thing I plan to do is to take her shopping for a wedding dress. I love you, but I am not particularly happy about this."

"Oh come on," he goaded. "You know you're a little happy about this."

"I'm very happy you're happy, darlin' boy. But I sure don't like missing my own son's wedding. Now bring that girl home, so I can hug her neck."

"Will do, Momma. Will do. Poppa Bear, I am signing off."

"I'll take care of your momma. You go take care of your bride."

"Over and out."

Crain hung up. And then he did what turned out to be about the dumbest thing a man with a Texas A&M degree could do. He took the time to text everybody he knew, telling them he had married the cutest Ol' Miss Hotty Toddy ever found in Dallas. Yep, he was one happy groom. Right up until he made his bride a cup of coffee just the way she liked it—with a whole lot of sugar—and carried it into the bedroom.

"Sweetheart," he whispered, until he realized the bed was empty. "Sugar?" he yelled, looking around the room, his eyes coming to rest on the note written with her preferred red Sharpie. "Honey?" he said, moving forward to pick up the note.

Four little words. Four little words Crain Carraway had no idea what to do with. Four little words that left him certain of absolutely nothing.

I'm sorry – cold feet.

Help others find
Taming Molly
by leaving a review at your favorite retailer.
Your time and effort is very much appreciated.

Liz Kelly Books

All of my Heroes of Henderson novels and novellas are complete romances in and of themselves and do not need to be read in any particular order. However, it's a little more fun that way.

Taming Molly and *Tempting Vivi* are part of The DuVal Cousins series showcasing Lolly's Henderson cousins as heroines of their own stories.

Heroes of Henderson full-length Novels

Good Cop
Bad Cop
Top Dog
Tempting Vivi
Under Dog - *Coming in 2015*

Heroes of Henderson Novellas

Playin' Cop
Taming Molly

For more information and excerpts from all my novels, please visit my website: www.LizKellyBooks.com and sign up for my newsletter to learn about future releases.

About the Author

Growing up every summer in a place where dancing and romancing are literally part of its theme song, Liz Kelly can't help but be a romantic at heart. And since her favorite author, Kathleen E. Woodiwiss wrote some of the world's greatest romances, she's just trying to give the world a little more of that. (Okay, maybe a little sexier that, but we are now in a new millennium after all.)

A graduate of Wake Forest University, where she met her handsome golf-addicted husband, (who is now sporting dark glasses everywhere he goes) Liz is a mother of two grown sons (also sporting dark glasses) and a miniature Labradoodle named Isabelle. They split their time between The Windy City of Chicago and the Fountain of Youth, a.k.a. Naples, FL where dancing and romancing continues on ad infinitum.